D1401287

For my babies, Isobel and Tom -D.B.

To my baby, Freddie -R.B.

tiger tales
an imprint of ME Media, LLC
5 River Road, Suite 128, Wilton, CT 06897
Published in the United States 2012
Originally published in Great Britain 2011
by Egmont UK Limited
Text copyright © 2011 David Bedford
Illustrations copyright © 2011 Rosalind Beardshaw
Hardcover ISBN-13: 978-1-58925-108-3
Hardcover ISBN-10: 1-58925-108-3
Paperback ISBN-13: 978-1-58925-435-0
Paperback ISBN-10: 1-58925-435-X
Printed in Singapore
TWP0611
1 3 5 7 9 10 8 6 4 2

For more insight and activities,
visit us at www.tigertalesbooks.com

NEWARK NY 14513

Mole's

Babies

by David Bedford
Illustrated by Rosalind Beardshaw

tiger tales

One warm, sunny day,
Morris found Mini clearing out their molehill.

"We need to make
more room," said
Mini. "Our babies
are coming soon!"

Morris the mole loved babies.

"Yippee!" he said,

and he hurried down
from the hill to
get ready.

The barnyard was full of **happy** babies.

Morris wanted to make his babies happy, too.

But how?
Morris looked more
closely and saw . . .

bunnies.

Hoppy, floppy bunnies.

Morris watched the hoppy, floppy bunnies *hopping* in the field with their dad.

The bunnies were **happy.**

"oppy babies are **happy** babies," said Morris.

And he began hopping, too,

so that he could learn how.

But it wasn't long before . . .

Morris hopped too high!

He landed on his nose.
"Ouch!"

"Are you all right, Morris?"
called Mini, from the top
of the molehill.

"I think so," said Morris,
rubbing his nose.

"Good," said Mini,
"because our babies
are on their way!"

"Yippee!" said Morris,
and he hurried off again
to get ready.

This time
he saw . . .

chicks.

Chirpy,

chirpy

chicks.

Morris watched the chirpy, chirpy chicks

flapping in the nest with their dad.

The chicks were **happy.**

Flappy babies
are **happy** babies,"
said Morris.

And he began
flapping, too,

so that he could
learn how.

But it wasn't long before . . .

Morris **flapped** and **flopped** off the branch!

He tumbled to the ground
and landed on his head.
"Ouch!"

"Are you all right, Morris?"
called Mini, from the
top of the molehill.

"Good," said Mini,
"because our
babies are
nearly here!"

"Yippee!"
said Morris,
and he hurried off
once more
to get ready.

This time
he saw . . .

"I think so,"
said Morris, rubbing his head.

ducklings.

Quacky, quacky ducklings.

Morris watched the quacky, quacky ducklings
splashing in the pond with their dad.

The ducklings were **happy**.

"Splashy babies are **happy** babies," said Morris.

And he began splashing, too,
so that he could learn how.

But it wasn't long before . . .

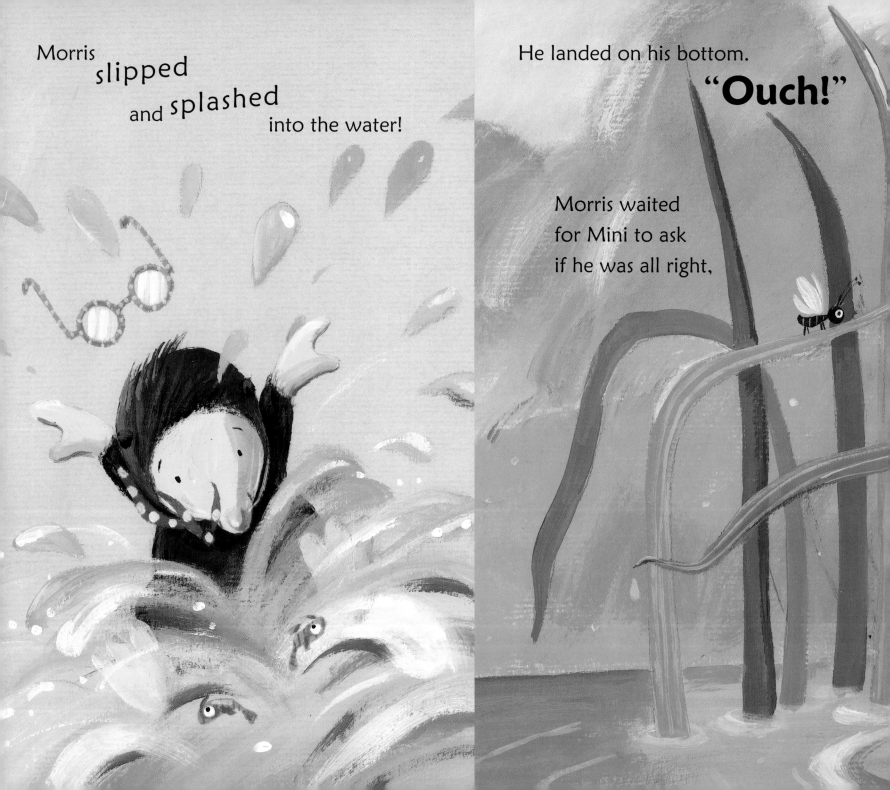

Morris **slipped** and **splashed** into the water!

He landed on his bottom.

"Ouch!"

Morris waited for Mini to ask if he was all right,

but Mini was nowhere
to be seen.

Morris walked slowly back to
his molehill and sat down.

"My babies are coming
and I am not ready,"
he said to himself.

"Hopping makes happy babies.

Flapping makes happy babies.

And splashing makes happy babies.

But I cannot do ANY of those things."

Then a voice from deep inside
the molehill said,

"Our babies
don't NEED
any of
those things,
Morris!"

"Our
babies
only
need . . .

The mole babies kissed and cuddled with their dad.
Morris, Mini, and their babies were **happy!**

And for ever after.

"Love makes happy babies!" said Morris.

And he gave his babies
all the *love* they would ever need.

If you liked this story, why not read
the first book about Morris?

Morris is looking for love, but when he
heads down to the farm, what he finds
at the end of his nose isn't quite what
he was expecting.

Hardcover ISBN: 978-1-58925-417-6
Paperback ISBN: 978-1-58925-417-1